Lily, Lana, and The Exploricorn

L and R sounds

By Cass Kim, M.A. CCC-SLP
Illustrated by Kawena VK

D1567350

Lily, Lana, and The Exploricorn
L and R sounds
P.A.C.B. Speech Sounds Series

This is a work of fiction. Names, characters, places, and incidents either are the product of the author's imagination or are used fictitiously. Any resemblance to actual persons, living or dead, events, or locales is entirely coincidental.

Copyright © 2021 Cass Kim
All rights reserved. No part of this book may be reproduced or used in any manner without written permission of the copyright owner except for the use of quotations in a book review. For more information, email: casskimslp@pacbspeech.org
Cover Design by: Kawena VK
Illustrations by: Kawena VK
Illustration Non-Commercial Use Copyright: Kawena VK
Illustration Commercial Use Copyright: Cass Kim

Join us at PACBSpeech.org to find the entire line of books and products!

P.A.C.B.

Phonological and Articulation Children's Books
Learning Speech — Together

I'm Lily! This is my dog Lana. She's a golden retriever mix and my best friend.

We live with my grandma in North Dakota. You can see her on the porch, by the easel. She's an artist and today she's painting this field of sunflowers.

When she's outside painting, Lana and I get to play in the field, eat a picnic, and read or color. Sometimes I have to do homework — including my speech practice!

Sometimes my tongue gets a little stuck when I try to say Lana's name, or even my own sometimes. It makes her name like Wanna ... which might be a little silly since I've never heard any dog named that before.

La, la, la, Lana... and Lily!

I've found that if I touch my tongue tip up behind my teeth first, and then draw my lips into an almost-smile, with the air flowing around my tongue, it comes out pretty well.

La, la, la, Lana...and Lily!

I like to practice curling my tongue back, too, for the strong R in some words. Lana loves it when I read to her to practice my speech!

Lana and I were just reading a book all about unicorns, but we finished it now.

It's been a fun and busy day, so now we're going to stare up at the clouds and see what creatures we can see.

Do you ever do that? I like when I see things like narwhals, and lions, and giraffes. Animals Lana and I only ever see in a zoo or a book usually.

What creatures do you see in the clouds?

As I'm staring up at the sky suddenly...I see... a big shadow!

It has four legs...

A long body...

A tail and a mane...

And.....is that...is that a horn?

I sit straight up and look at the unicorn in front of me.
Lana is sitting next to me, wagging her tail.
If she's not scared, I guess I'm not scared either!

This unicorn looks a little different than I expected.
It isn't pink or purple or really very rainbowy.

It leans its head down low, inching the tip of its horn toward my
forehead. I hold my breath as it comes slowly closer and closer.

As it touches its horn to my forehead, the green and yellow field around us fades away and Lana and I are in a whole new place, filled with sand...and...cactuses?

"Where are we?"

"Well," Lana answers, "we're in part of the Sonoran Desert in California."

"You can talk!? And where did you get those glasses?" I am simply shocked.

"The Exploricorn gave them to me." Lana grins her happy smile, her tail wagging rapidly. "Each ring of its horn will take us to a new place to explore."

The sun is quite hot as I look around. I see so many creatures and plants I have never seen before.

What can you see?

I see a...

Barrel cactus

And a...

Gila monster...

Also a big hairy tarantula!

Over there, I see an ironwood tree

And a roadrunner!

It's amazing how I magically know all of these creatures.

"Of course," says Lana, "that's the magic of the Exploricorn. Touch the blue ring on the horn and see where we will go."

As suddenly as we were in the desert,
we are now surrounded by snow and ice and
a big dark sky filled with dancing lights.
Luckily, we are magically dressed for
the frozen world we have entered.

"Where are we now?" I look expectantly at Lana,
whose glasses have turned into snowmobile goggles.

"Somewhere near Fairbanks, Alaska. That show in the
sky is the Aurora Borealis...or the Northern Lights."

"Wow! It's so beautiful!"

It takes some work, but as the sky lightens a little,
I drag my gaze to look around me and see...

A moose....

And a....

Black bear.

I look to the river and see the flash of scales as salmon swim hard against the river current.

"They usually run up the stream in the summer, but the Exploricorn thought you might like to see them." High above, an eagle soars past us.

Turning, I look toward the ocean in
the distance, I think I can see...

Look! An orca jumping in the waves.

A seal...

And a polar bear!

Those trees lining the edge of the forest are spruce trees...and some paper birch trees, too.

"Try the dark green swirl on its horn next." Lana wags her tail next to the Exploricorn, who dips the horn low so I can reach out and put a finger on the green ring.

Suddenly we're in a swampy land with many trees. Lana is wearing waders, and I am also dry because of my own high rubber boots and overalls.

Before I can even ask her, Lana tells me, "Welcome to the bayou of Louisiana."

The first thing I see is a big, spikey turtle sunning itself on a rock. An alligator snapping turtle. I will be keeping my hands very far from its mouth!

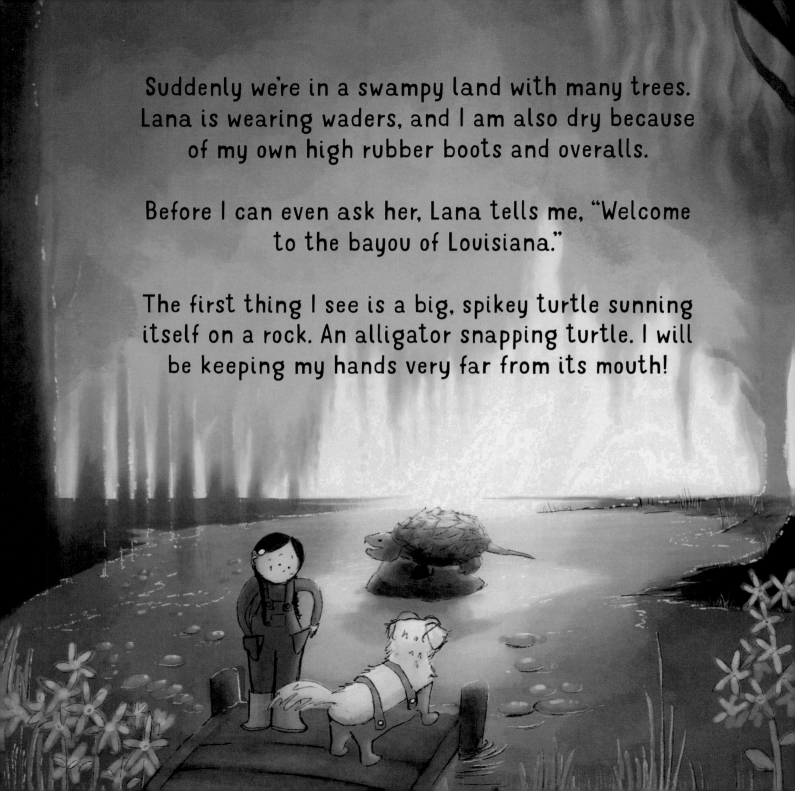

I can see a beautiful blue flower,
the Louisiana Bluestar.

I also see lots of little critters along
the banks of the muddy water...

A racoon.

And a...

Muskrat next to a mink!

I also see a deer bending for a drink and...

Oh no!

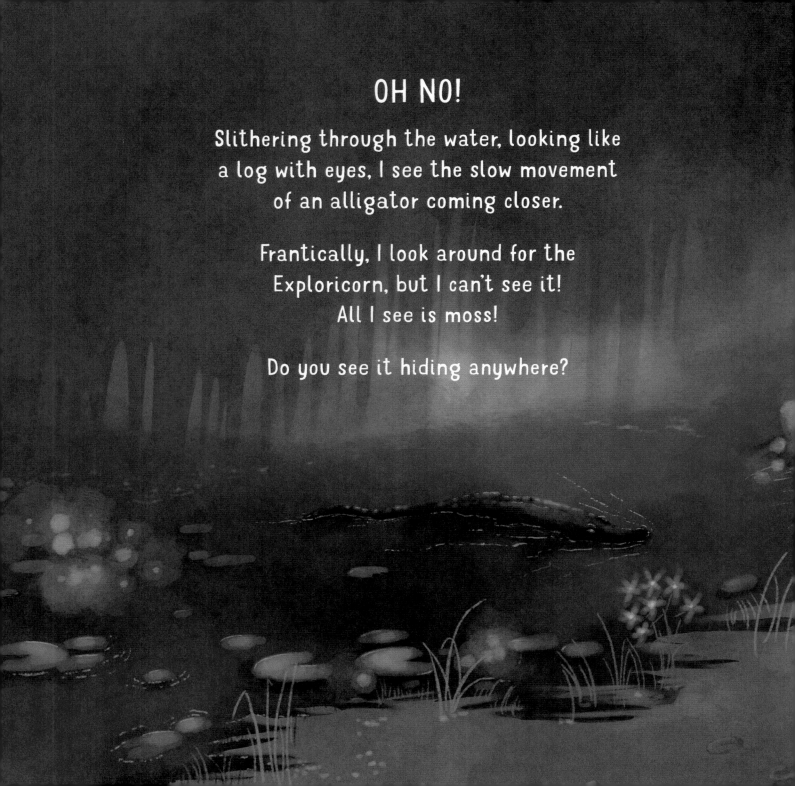

OH NO!

Slithering through the water, looking like
a log with eyes, I see the slow movement
of an alligator coming closer.

Frantically, I look around for the
Exploricorn, but I can't see it!
All I see is moss!

Do you see it hiding anywhere?

Lana whimpers slightly, and leans against my legs as the gator's tail sweeps it closer still...

"Lily, honey."
I hear my grandma's voice!
Just as the gator starts to open his mouth,
I hear her again.
"Lily, time to wake up."

My eyes snap open, and there I am, back in
North Dakota, a sleeping Lana snuggled close
to me on our blanket in the sunflower field.

Phew! It was only a dream.

And yet... it might be fun to meet a
real Exploricorn, don't you think?

The End

About the Author: Cass Kim

Cass Kim is an established young adult author. She is best known for creating the "Autumn Nights" Charity Anthology Series, as well as the "Wilders" Young Adult trilogy. In addition to her work as an author, Cass is a practicing Speech-Language Pathologist with a decade of experience. She holds her Certificate of Clinical Competency from the American Speech and Hearing Association, as well as a master's degree from Central Michigan University.

About the Illustrator: Kawena VK

Kawena VK grew up in Hawaii with a great fascination for art and nature. She learned through a traditional atelier at the Windward Community College where she was inspired, by her college instructor, to pursue art. She later received her Bachelor of Arts from the University of Hawaii. With her family and friends, Kawena has found a deep sense of happiness through her love for drawing and painting.

Helpful Tips for Parents:

L and R are two of the most difficult sounds to work on. They take a lot of practice, so doing extra work at home is especially important for these two sounds. Until new research was completed in 2019, the expected age for R and L development was 6 or later. Now we know that most children should be mastering L closer to age 4, and R closer to age 5. Don't hesitate to request a speech therapy appointment for your child even if some people are saying it's too early. Earlier is always better.

R can be made in two different ways, and both of them are hard for children to see. The first is how Lily talks about it in the book — the tongue tip touching the roof of the mouth. The other way is "bunched" with the back of the tongue bunched up (almost like Mountain Tongue from Greg and His Gecko) and the tip of the tongue brushing the back of the lower teeth.

Both ways that the R is made require the back of the tongue to be wide enough for the edges to touch the upper back molars. Sometimes I play "Pointy Tongue, Flat Tongue" where kids look at themselves and practice making their tongue long and narrow, and then short and flat. A selfie app and some funny filters (we like animal and monster faces) can really increase the fun factor for this game.

Because R can be so hard to see and to say, using non-words at first can be a good way to practice. Purrrring like a cat, grrrowling like a dog, or vrrrooming like a car are lower pressure ways to practice the tongue placement while playing.

Another way I sometimes shape R for little ones that make the W sound instead is to practice the way their lips look. W is very round, and not what we want for R. R should be a little wider, more boxy. Starting from Shh and moving to R can help, with words like Share, Sharp, Shore.

L is another sound that relies on the right lip movements. Sometimes little ones will have their tongue in the place until they say a word - then their lips try to take over. I work on "smile" talking with them, using a mirror. We practice talking through a smile, to keep their lips nice and wide — and make their tongue do the work. This can make for some really funny moments, and I often have them quote their favorite movies or shows to keep it fun.

The tongue placement for L is a lot like the tongue taps in Ted and Tina Adopt a Kitten – the tongue tip should be on the gum ridge behind the upper front teeth. Sometimes it will barely tap, other times it may rest there a little longer, more like the N than the T ("Lily" is all taps, "full" might be more of a hold).

Talking about how your tongue and lips move as you say these words, and exaggerating the movements, can really help the sounds come together for little ones. Once in a while, it helps to check in with them and ask them how their own tongue and lips are moving. Getting them thinking about how they move their mouth to speak is often the first step in therapy. Having them think about their own movements and sounds while speaking is part of getting the sounds right outside of the therapy room.

Practicing can be frustrating for children, especially if they're really struggling. Adding in an active component can sometimes take the focus off the frustration (and let them vent a little steam in a healthy way). Kicking a soccer ball, jumping hopscotch, or practicing basketball shots every 2-3 words can be a good mix of work and play.

Did you know that vision and hearing problems greatly impact speech learning? If your child is struggling to produce sounds, reduced vision or multiple ear infections may be a factor. This is something to bring up to your pediatrician.

These books are not intended to be a substitute for skilled speech therapy treatment. They are meant to be a supplemental addition to practice at home, and a way for families to work together on sound production activities and early literacy skills. If you are concerned about your child's speech, please ask your school system and your pediatrician for a speech therapy evaluation.

Don't forget to stop by our website for free activities. We will continue to add new items, including our free early learning activity printable worksheets.

Please take a moment to leave a review for this book and the series on Amazon. It really makes an enormous difference for our small business.

FOR MORE INFORMATION ON SPEECH SOUND DEVELOPMENT AND HOW READING IMPACTS
SPEECH DEVELOPMENT, VISIT: HTTPS://WWW.PACBSPEECH.ORG/HOME
CHECK US OUT ON INSTAGRAM! @P.A.C.B.SPEECH

Made in the USA
Middletown, DE
11 June 2024

55605041R00018